*Reissued on the Occasion of
the 50th Anniversary of Little Golden Books*

DOCTOR DAN

THE BANDAGE MAN

By
Helen Gaspard
Pictures by
Corinne Malverne

A GOLDEN BOOK • NEW YORK
Western Publishing Company, Inc.,
Racine, Wisconsin 53404

A Note from the Publishers

For a long, long time, the publishers have been ardent admirers of BAND-AID Adhesive Bandages—not only for themselves (publishers seem to cut themselves more than other people) but because of their effect on children. We've noted that BAND-AID Adhesive Bandages not only cheer and comfort small boys and girls who bang themselves up, but that they make wonderful playthings as well. No one quite knows how many millions of dolls and stuffed toys and live pets have been patched up in this manner.

Consequently, when the idea for this book came to us, we promptly went to Johnson & Johnson and asked them if they would be willing to help us. They were very nice about it and asked that we point out that BAND-AID is Johnson & Johnson's trademark for its brand of adhesive bandages and for several other products in its line.

This book is for Richard Peter

© 1950 Western Publishing Company, Inc. Copyright renewed 1977. All rights reserved. Printed in the U.S.A. No part of this book may be reproduced or copied in any form without written permission from the publisher. All trademarks are the property of Western Publishing Company, Inc. Library of Congress Catalog Card Number: 91-77809 ISBN: 0–307–00142–3   R MCMXCII

D AN is a busy fellow. He is always on the go. But one day in a big back-yard cowboy fight he fell and scratched his finger on his make-believe gun.

And what do you think the big cowboy did?
He cried.

"Boo hoo hoo," Dan cried. And he ran in the
house to his mother.

Now his mother was always glad to see Dan.
But a cowboy crying? How could that be?

"Why, that's nothing to cry over," Mother
said when she saw the bright red spot.

"We'll wash it clean with soap and water and
bandage it up, and it will be better than new."
And quick as a wink, it was!

Back went Dan to the cowboy fight. And all
the boys gathered around to see his new clean
bandage, too.

Next day Dan hitched up Spotty his pup to take his sister Carly's doll for a ride.

But Spotty saw a cat he wanted to chase, and he forgot all about that doll.

Lickety split, Spotty started off!

The wagon tipped over. The doll tumbled out. And Carly started to cry, "My baby hurt herself," because the doll had a bump on her head.

"This is nothing to cry over," said brother
Dan. "I know just what to do."

So he led Spotty and Carly into the house.
And he carried the hurt little doll himself, with
a rather bad bump on her head.

"We'll wash it clean," said Dan.
And he did.
"We'll bandage it up." And he did that, too.

He pulled out the little string on the bandage wrap. He picked the bandage out and held the two stiff pieces. And zip! that bandage was on the doll's head.

"There!" smiled Dan. "She's better than new."

"Now," said Carly. "I want one, too."

"Are you hurt?" asked Dan.

"I don't know," Carly said, looking for a scratch. And sure enough, she found one. It was a very tiny scratch, and rather old, but it was a scratch just the same.

Dan washed it clean and bandaged it up.
"Thank you," said Carly. "It's better than
new."

"Woof!" said Spotty, and held up his paw.

Dan laughed. "I guess you must want a bandage, too."

So he put one on Spotty's paw.

Next day Daddy was home from work. He
went out to mow the lawn. And what do you
think? He cut his finger on a slippery-sharp
lawn mower blade!

"Let me fix you up, Dad," said Dan. "I know what to do. We'll wash your finger clean and bandage it up, and it will be better than new."

Dad looked surprised, but he followed Dan.
And soon Dad wore a bandage, too.

"You're a handy fellow to have around," said Dad. And he shook Dan's hand. "I have a new name for you. We'll call you Doctor Dan, the Bandage Man."

And they do to this day. So we will, too.

Some day, perhaps, you or one of your toys may get bumped or cut or scratched. When that happens, you can really use one of the BAND-AID Adhesive Bandages in the front of this book.